Published by
Vegan Publishers
Beverly, MA
www.veganpublishers.com

Cover art and design by Carlos Patiño
Book design by Carlos Patiño

ISBN: 978-1-940184-01-2
Library of Congress Control Number: 2013914187

Printed and bound by Tien Wah Press (Pte) Ltd,
October 2013, in Malaysia.

DAVE LOVES CHICKENS

written & illustrated by Carlos Patiño

Este libro esta dedicado a la persona mas especial en mi vida - Monique

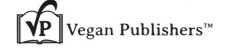
Vegan Publishers™

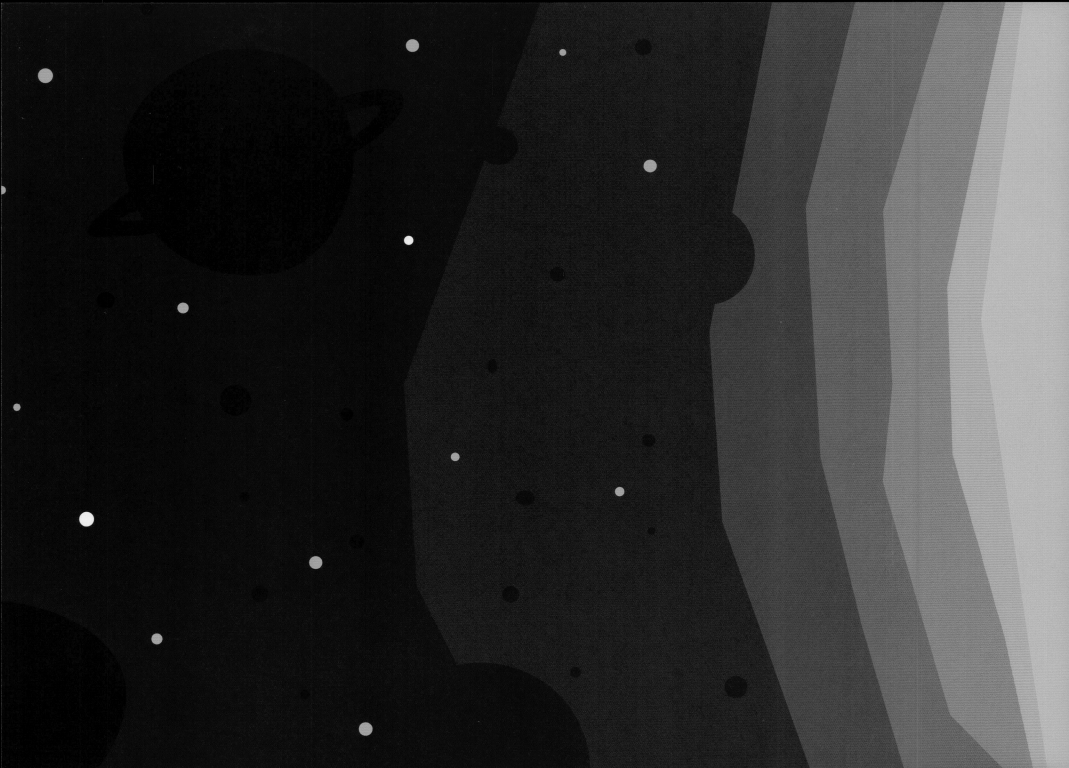

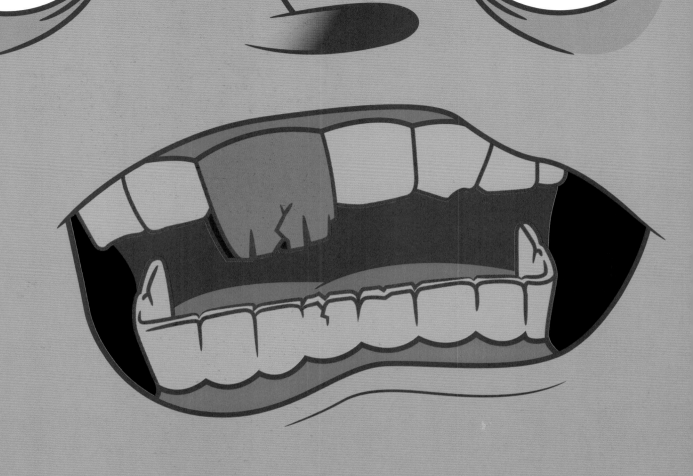

AND A TOOTH THAT'S

OLD

DAVE
IS A VERY
SMART MONSTER

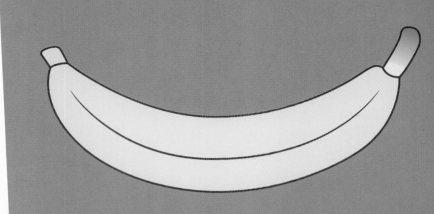

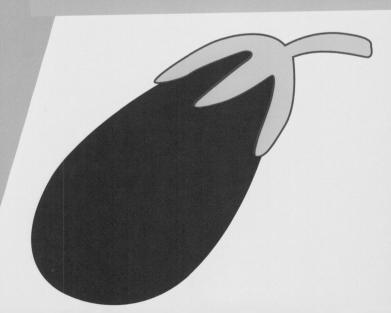

WHEN IT COMES TO
HIS MEATLESS DIET

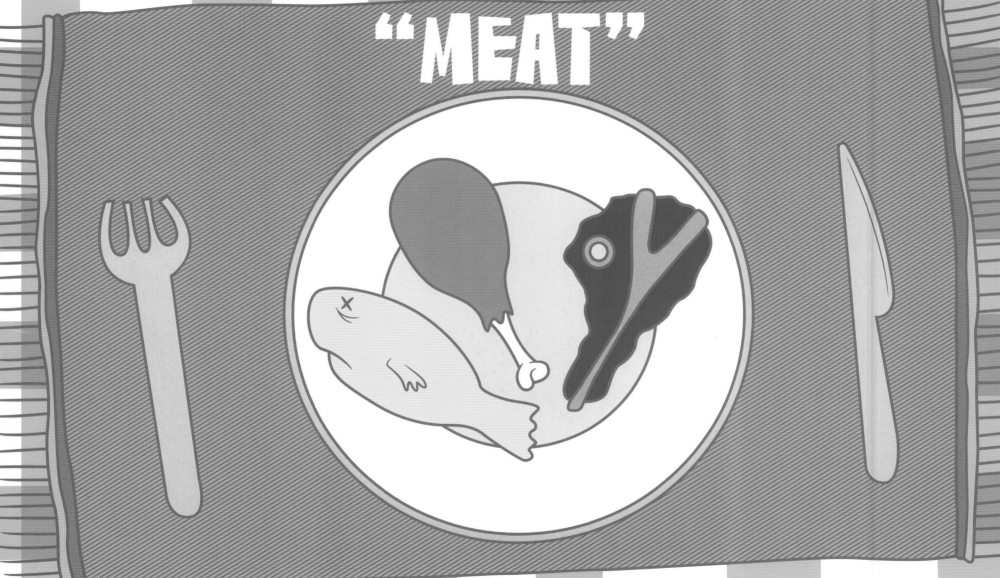

CHICKENS FOR EXAMPLE

THEY ARE **NOT** FOR US TO SAMPLE

THEY ENJOY A DUST BATH

TO FEED THEIR
GROWING CHICKEN
BRAINS

ANY CHICKEN DESERVES TO LIVE FROM 5 TO 11 YEARS

A LIFE SPAN AS LONG AS A WHITE-TAILED DEER'S

CHICKENS CAN TRAVEL UP TO 9 MILES PER HOUR

WHILE SMILING ABOUT THEIR SPEED AND POWER

…AND WILL PROUDLY SHOW YOU THEIR MUSCLES FLEX

SO WHY IS EATING THEM NOT BANNED?

AND ALL LIVING THINGS HAVE A RIGHT TO BE FREE